DEBORAH GOULD

GRANDPA'S SLIDE SHOW

Illustrated by Cheryl Harness

Lothrop, Lee & Shepard Books   New York

First Edition 1 2 3 4 5 6 7 8 9 10

Library of Congress Cataloging in Publication Data Gould, Deborah Lee. Grandpa's slide show. Summary: Whenever they visit Grandpa, Sam and Douglas always watch a slide show. After Grandpa dies, they watch the show to remember him. [1. Grandfathers—Fiction. 2. Death—Fiction] I. Harness, Cheryl, ill. II. Title. PZ7.G723Gr 1987 [E] 86-20981 ISBN 0-688-06972-X ISBN 0-688-06973-8 (lib. bdg.)

For Bernard S. Lee
Thanks to Janet Kamien
—D. G.

To Uri and Current, folks and friends
—C. H.

One thing always happened whenever Sam and his little brother, Douglas, stayed overnight at their grandparents' house. That was Grandpa's slide show. After supper Grandpa always asked Sam to turn out all the lights in the living room. Both boys settled with Grandma on the pillowed sofa while Grandpa sat in a wooden chair behind the slide projector. Grandpa loaded the projector with one of his many carousels of slides. He adjusted everything until the blurry patches of color on the wall turned into one clear picture. Grandpa's slide show had begun.

The first slide beamed vacation sunlight into the nighttime room. Sometimes in the first slide Douglas, Sam, and Mom sat smiling at a picnic table. Other times Grandma and Grandpa stood together at a mountain lookout, or Uncle Carl and his girls waved from a Ferris wheel.

Once the first slide was in place, Grandpa handed the control device to Sam. Then in a careful voice Grandpa said, "Next slide, please." Sam pressed the forward button on the control device, and a new slide appeared on the wall.

Sometimes they watched slide after slide of fruit trees or old houses. Sam didn't mind. He loved pressing the forward button and hearing each slide drop, *click-clack,* into place.

Sam liked the slide show for another reason, too. He knew
many people in the slides, but he hadn't known them when
the pictures were taken. There was a slide of Uncle Carl and
Mom as children in a wooden sandbox. "That was in the
backyard of our first house," said Grandma. She had
something to say about almost every slide.

There was one of a thin, dark-haired man standing by a statue in a park. "That was Grandpa in 1947, I think," said Grandma. Now Grandpa's hair was almost white and he was bigger around the middle.

There was Grandma as a smiling young woman leaning against a large tree. "The first picture Grandpa ever took of me," explained Grandma.

Grandpa nodded. During the show he never said much except, "Next slide, please."

Finally an empty patch of light shone bright against the wall. Then Grandpa would say, "That's the whole carousel." At once Sam and Douglas scooted forward and made shadow puppets until Grandpa flipped off the projector light. "Good night, boys," he said. "I'm tired. Aren't you?" After hugging both boys, he would lean back on the sofa to rest.

Then Grandma helped Sam and Douglas get ready for bed.
Once they were in bed, she read them story after story. She
read until the stories turned into dreams.

One time Sam and Douglas came to stay overnight, but there was no slide show. Mom came with them because Grandpa was very ill. He was in the hospital. Grandma had spent many hours there with him.

That evening Mom visited Grandpa at the hospital while Grandma made supper and helped the boys get ready for bed. She read story after story, and Douglas fell asleep. Sam lay awake. He watched Grandma stand up.

"Are you going back to the hospital tonight?" he whispered.

"Yes," said Grandma, "when your mom gets back."

"Can I visit Grandpa at the hospital tomorrow?" he asked.

"Maybe for a little while," she answered.

Later that night, when Grandma was at the hospital, Grandpa died. Mom told Sam and Douglas early the next morning. Her voice sounded funny. Douglas acted silly. He couldn't believe it. Sam didn't want to believe it, but he knew it was true.

Grandma and Mom took turns calling to tell friends and relatives that Grandpa was dead. They planned a funeral for the next day. They said they would do things with the boys, but phone calls and strange visitors interrupted all day long. One call was from Dad. "I'll come early tomorrow morning," he told them.

Douglas acted sillier and sillier. Sam scolded him. Then Douglas acted cranky. Sam knew what to do. Together they made a secret fort with blankets in the guest room. They filled it with every toy they could find. They came out when Grandma called, "Suppertime." Her friend Harriet had made meatballs, rice, and apple pie. Everything tasted odd. It wasn't like Grandma's food.

After supper Sam asked, "Will we ever have a slide show again?"

"Yes, but not tonight," said Grandma. She put both arms around Sam and let him cry close to her.

The next morning Dad came. He took the boys to a playground. "This is our chance to run around," he said. "At the funeral we'll need to act calm."

The funeral home was crowded with Grandpa's friends and relatives. Sam recognized some of them from the slide shows. During the ceremony people sat in rows. Some gave short speeches about Grandpa. Someone asked for a minute of

silence so each person could think about him. Sam only
stared at the polished wood casket and wondered how
Grandpa looked inside. He pictured a sad gray face. He
squeezed his fists together to make the picture leave his mind.

After the ceremony everyone came to the house. They stood around with drinks and plates of food. The grown-ups talked louder and louder. They hugged each other. They sat together and laughed at stories about the past.

The only other children around were Uncle Carl's girls. They were both several years older than Sam and Douglas. The four of them played board games and watched television in the guest room. Dad joined them for a while. "The kids are quieter than the grown-ups today," he joked.

The house was crowded until dark. Gradually people began leaving. Finally Dad had to leave, too. "But I'll see you again in two days," he promised when they hugged good-bye.

Now the only people in the house were Grandma, Mom, Douglas, and Sam. Harriet had left them a cheese casserole for supper. Sam and Douglas ate some, but Mom and Grandma just sat with the boys and drank tea. Mom told a story about Grandpa building a sandbox when she was little. Sam asked, "Can we do the slide show tonight?"

"Yes, I'd like that," said Grandma, "if you and your mom will handle the projector."

Together Sam and Mom set up the projector in the living room. They chose a carousel of slides labeled "Miscellaneous Vacations."

Mom sat behind the projector as Grandpa had, and Sam sat nearby on the sofa ready to press the forward button. Grandma and Douglas turned out the lights and settled in next to him.

"Here goes," said Mom, and the first slide flashed on the wall. "Oh, these are from way back," said Mom. "That's our first trip to Canada, when I was nine and Carl was twelve."

“And I was thirty-five,” added Grandma. In the slide Grandma and her two children stood together on a boat dock. They smiled and squinted in the bright sun.

“Press the forward button, Sam,” urged Mom.

“Grandpa always said, ‘Next slide, please,’” Sam told her.

“Sam, it can’t be exactly the way Grandpa did it,” Mom warned him, but she did say, “Next slide, please.”

The next five slides were from the Canada trip. The next seven were farms and mountains in Virginia. After Grandma said something about each one, Mom said, "Next slide, please." Then Sam pressed the forward button and listened for the firm *click-clack*.

The next slide showed Grandma in sunglasses on the deck of a ferry. "That's recent," said Grandma, surprised. "Our trip to Nantucket last summer."

The slide after that showed Grandpa on the same ferry. He was frowning. Suddenly Douglas ran forward toward the picture. "Don't be mad, Grandpa," he shouted. He patted Grandpa's picture on the wall, so it appeared unevenly on his hand.

"Douglas, go back to Grandma," Mom said firmly.

"He wasn't angry, Douggy. I think the sun was in his eyes," Grandma explained.

"Maybe we should stop now," Mom said.

"No, go on, dear, it's interesting," said Grandma, pulling Douglas back next to her.

Finally they came to the last slide and then the bright patch of light. "That's the whole carousel," called Douglas sleepily.

"A good show," said Grandma, nodding her thanks to Sam and Mom. Then she stood up, announcing, "All right, boys, bed and story now, as usual."

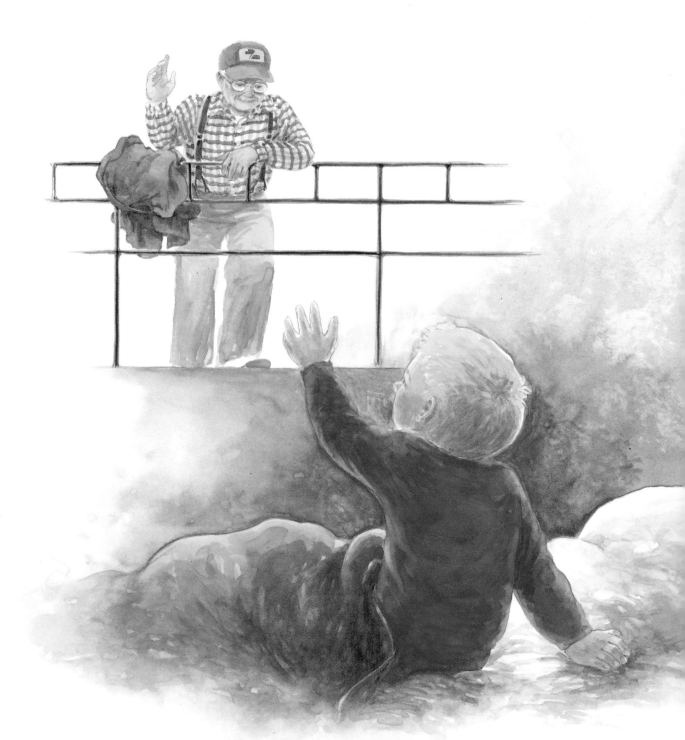

That night Grandma read to them in a soft slow voice. Before her second story was over, Sam's dream began. In the dream Grandpa waved to Sam from the ferry. Sam waved back. He could see that Grandpa was smiling.